A BLINK IS AS GOOD AS A WINK

Lois Collins Kerr

Written and Illustrated by: Lois Collins Kerr

A SPENCER FAMILY BOOKS PRODUCTION

LIFEVEST PUBLISHING, INC.
Centennial, Colorado

A Blink Is As Good As A Wink
written and illustrated by Lois Collins Kerr
Copyright 2007 © Lois Collins Kerr

Published and Printed by:
Lifevest Publishing
4901 E. Dry Creek Rd., #120
Centennial, CO 80122
www.lifevestpublishing.com

Printed in the United States of America
I.S.B.N. 1-59879-452-3

This book is dedicated to my father, Richard Collins, who taught me to wink

Thank you for choosing
Spencer Family Books

Starting with Zanita Spencer Collins, who began teaching in a one-room schoolhouse in 1929, Spencer Family Books includes three generations and six family members with an incredible amount of talent and experience among them and a strong commitment to produce high-quality children's books.

Visit us at **www.spencerfamilybooks.com** to learn more and to order the wonderful children's stories available from Spencer Family Books.

Daddy says a blink is when you close both eyes for just a little while and then open them. A wink is when you close one eye for just a little while and leave the other eye open.

Daddy is very good at winking, but I am not. I try and try, but I can't make one eye stay open when the other one closes. Daddy says, "Don't worry, Richard, just keep trying and you will be able to do it someday. Right now, a blink is as good as a wink."

A wink can be a special, secret way to say things without speaking. When it was Mommy's birthday, I had a present for her, and Daddy said, "Keep Mommy's present hidden and, when I wink, you can go get it and bring it to her for a surprise."

I think Muffin, the cat, can wink or, maybe, one eye can sleep while the other eye stays awake.

Our dog, Winston, never opens his eyes all the way. He can blink but he can't wink.

Amber, the fish, never closes her eyes. She can't blink or wink.

My baby sister, Rylie, can do three things. She can hold her eyes open very wide and stare or she can close them when she is sleeping or she can shut them very tight when she cries. Rylie can't wink.

The very best one at winking is my Grandpa. When he winks, one eyebrow goes down and one side of his moustache goes up.

When Daddy drops me off at Busy Bees, which is my class at school, he always gives me a wink "Goodbye" and I try to wink back. The only one who can wink at Busy Bees is my teacher, Miss Alfie. She can wink with either eye.

Today was different! Today when Daddy winked goodbye in my classroom,

I winked back!

I did it! I winked!

Daddy was so surprised, he blinked.

A BLINK IS AS GOOD AS A WINK

by **Lois Collins Kerr**
A SPENCER FAMILY BOOKS PRODUCTION

I.S.B.N. 1-59879-452-3

Order Online at:
www.authorstobelievein.com

By Phone Toll Free at:
1-877-843-1007